Opera Goats

By

Gordon Goodman

ISBN: 0-9746027-9-5
Imaginings Publications
Los Angeles USA

DEDICATION

To my parents.

CONTENTS

ACKNOWLEDGMENTS

Frita Von Frikt would like to thank her voice teacher, Madame Klump. Ms. Frikt does not think Madame Klump was a very good teacher, nor does she seem to care about the woman in the least. Yet, Ms. Frikt insists we add an acknowledgement to give readers the impression that she is a kind and caring person. Plus, she threatened us with bodily harm.

PROLOGUE

Before we begin this tale, there are a few terms that need explanation. They are theatre terms. If you memorize these, people will undoubtedly think that you are intimate with the arts and with the stage in particular. Either that, or they will assume you are pitifully desperate to impress them with useless trivia and will make an effort to never go to the theatre with you again.

That said, let us proceed...

An "understudy" is a performer who knows all the words and songs of a starring performer. The understudy is there in case something happens to the starring performer. For this reason, the understudy may hope something DOES happen to the starring performer. The understudy takes and injured star's place because "the show must go on."

This phrase, "the show must go on," was originated by people who put up the money for show. Very simply, "the show must go on", or people lose money. So, out of the goodness of their hearts, the role of understudy was created. Stars usually associate with understudies just enough to let them know, "Yes, I am in fine health, thank you. Please stop asking."

"Props" are the things put on the stage. Props can be lamps, books, tables, chairs or even fake spears or swords. Sometimes props can be people, or at least some actors feel that way. Props can also be food, but it is best not to eat this food, because you neither know where it has been, or for how long it has been there.

An "Opera Board", like most Boards should be, is usually a group of very rich people, or a group of people who are not rich, but have rich friends. The Opera Board runs the Opera and sees to it that:

1.Everyone gets paid and that…

2. There are spectacular parties to attract rich donors so that...

3. Everyone gets paid.

The "wings" refer to the right and left side of the stage. The actors wait in the wings, hidden by curtains, ready to make their entrance. Occasionally performers forget to make their entrance from the wings. This is not the fault of the construction of the wings, but rather the construction of the performer's brain.

The "orchestra pit" is the place in front of the stage where the musicians play music. It is usually lower than the stage so the audience can see over it. It is also a place where musicians do crossword puzzles when not playing an instrument.

"Sets" are fake walls and floors that sometimes can be moved during the show to make way for other sets. Sets make things quite livable and are often reminiscent of a college coffee house or tacky museum.

"Stagehands" do all the work on the stage. They set the props, set the lights, move the curtains and sets. In other words, they make the show happen. Stagehands are rarely seen, and dress accordingly. If they are seen during the show, you may feel a desire to scold them severely, as well as to caution them against their obviously habit of eating too much junk food.

"Catwalks" are ramps built high above the stage where stagehands stand and hang lights, scatter fake snow onto stage, and make sure ropes and wires are free and untangled. As you might imagine, it is very easy to fall from these catwalks, so it is not a place to wear platform heels.

A "backdrop" is usually a big canvas hung on a long heavy pipe that can be lowered or raised. The canvas normally has a picture painted on it. This picture helps make the audience believe the actors on stage are really someplace else. Up close, a backdrop smells very much like a kindergarten project.

The word "cast" refers to everyone in the show. This means the chorus and all the principal performers.

Performers love to be in a cast because it means they will have their picture in a program, which they can send home to their family, proving that they have not lost their minds. Unfortunately, with or without a program, most family members continue to believe they have.

If the show were a mighty sailing vessel, the "stage manager" would be its commander. He or she is the person who tells the stagehands, the lighting technician and the sound technician what to do and when to do it. Basically, this means that if anything goes wrong with the show, it will be the stage manager's fault. The stage manager, on the other hand, usually disagrees with this interpretation.

A "dresser" is a person who dresses the performers in their wonderful costumes. Sometimes a performer has very little time to change into a new outfit and needs help, so the dresser is there to peel off, zip up, straighten wigs, and guide the performer to their next entrance. Unfortunately, this is something most performers desperately need in real life.

An "audience" is a group of people who sit in the "house" and pay for expensive tickets to watch people who are paid to pretend the audience does not exist. In fact, the more an actor pretends the audience does not exist, the more the audience adores them. This is a conundrum, but there's very little to be done about it.

CHAPTER ONE

Farmer Tucci loved the Opera.

Oh, he loved his cows and his pigs and his chickens and his goats. He loved his wife Marta. But the music of the Opera filled his days.

A lot of Farmer Tucci's spending money, (the money his wife Marta would let him spend), went into buying wind-up phonograph players and records of all the great opera singers. He kept the records in his closet under his best suit, (which was his only suit), and under the shelf that held his wife's old sewing machine.

When the record players were wound up and spinning around, they looked like boxes with black pizzas twirling on top of them. While they would spin, the tip of a needle (which looked like a bird poking it's beak down on to the record) would scrape along making noise. This noise would come out a big horn that looked like a giant flower made of metal. And what finally came flowing out was the music that Farmer Tucci loved so well.

There was a record player in the house where he and Marta lived. There was a record player in the barn where he milked the cows. There was a record player in the shed where he fed the pigs. There was even a record player in the hen house where he picked up the green and brown eggs every morning. Every animal on Farmer Tucci's farm grew up listening to Opera.

It was what they heard the moment they were born. It was what they heard as the sun rose until the sun set. It was often what they heard as they slept.

The animals on the Tucci farm came to feel that things were not right with the world unless they heard the beautiful singing that came from those phonograph players day after day. So it went on the Tucci farm for many years.

Everyone in the countryside knew about the Tucci farm and it's beautiful cows, chickens, ducks, and goats, but the Tucci farm became best known because of their prize- winning pigs.

The pigs from the Tucci farm won ribbons and trophies and had their pictures taken with big flashes of smoke. They even had special costumes they would wear as they paraded through town on their way to be blessed at the church.

All the Tucci pigs would be dressed as some famous character in Opera. One year a pig might be dressed in a helmet, horns and a blond wig. Another year a pig might be dressed like a clown with a frilly collar. And every year they were blessed outside the church and Farmer Tucci would pray that his pigs would get even fatter than they were the year before.

It was a good life, but like everyone, Farmer Tucci dreamed of more. He dreamed of being at the opera instead of just listening to it on records.

Mrs. Tucci, Marta, dreamed of more too. She dreamed of having more money so she could buy the things she saw in magazines. "If I had extra money I know just what I would buy," she would always say to Farmer Tucci. "If I had extra money I would shop all day and buy nice dresses and nice pots and pans and especially a new sewing machine." But as it happened, they never seemed to have any extra money.

Farmer Tucci did his usual repairs on the barn, the henhouse, the shed, all the pens, and those repairs kept things together very well every year. But there are certain creatures living in the world that don't really care how much you repair things. In fact, they get very very fat by ruining things.

They are called termites. It was termites that decided to get very very fat on the shelf just above Farmer Tucci's records. In fact, it was termites that started this most magical and most musical of stories.

Termites look like ants, only termites don't like to live in the ground as ants do, and they don't like sunlight. Termites like to live in wood. Of course they have to eat the wood before they can live in it. So, the termites on Farmer Tucci's farm looked all over for the best wood in which to live, and decided the wood just above Farmer Tucci's records was about the best and tastiest wood they had ever seen.

One night, while Farmer Tucci snored and his wife Marta was fast asleep with curlers in her hair, there came a small "Crunch" sound from the closet. Then, there came a tiny "groaning" sound.

Just as Farmer Tucci let out another mighty snore, the shelf above the records...the shelf just above Farmer Tucci's one and only suit...the shelf holding Mrs. Tucci's sewing machine, came crashing down!

Farmer Tucci and his wife woke with a jolt!

Mrs. Tucci kept shouting, "The roof is falling! My goodness, it's the roof! It's falling!" Many of the animals on the farm woke, and hearing the loud crash, (or hearing Marta shout "The roof is falling"), began to "Moo", or "Baaa" or "Bagawk", or "Oink".

Farmer Tucci checked the roof. He checked every room. He looked out the window at the barn, but nothing was falling. Then he slid open the closet door.

It was the most horrible thing he had ever seen.

There on the floor of his closet, smashed to pieces by Marta's heavy sewing machine, was a mound of black plastic pieces, a mound of useless bits that used to be his beautiful collection of opera records.

Mrs. Tucci ran up beside him and started shrieking, seeing the hundreds of little termites scrambling to get back up the wall and out of the light.

Farmer Tucci didn't care about the termites. Staring at the mound of broken records that had taken him a lifetime to collect, he dropped to his knees, put his head in his hands and wept.

CHAPTER TWO

That morning, the sun rose in silence.

No phonographs were wound up.

No records were playing.

No opera singers were singing.

Farmer Tucci didn't come out to milk the cows, which made them very moody. He didn't come out to gather eggs, which made the hens scratch and scratch at the ground. The prize-winning pigs waited at the fence, but no sloshy, soupy food was poured into their trough. The goats stood waiting for their hay, but no flakes of hay came. Everyone waited. No one made a sound. It was the most uncomfortable feeling any of the animals had ever felt. They had grown up listening to music all their lives. Now they didn't know what to do. Something was very very wrong.

The sun felt bright and warm. Everything looked the normal. But nothing seemed quite as beautiful somehow. There was one goat, a young female goat, who felt this way more than the others.

Her name was Mimi.

Mimi was a milk goat. She was a French milk goat. Her parents were pureblooded French milk goats and had taught her that a French milk goat was by far better than any other goat in the world. Mimi made this very clear whenever the other goats passed by. She would never look at them, and stuck her nose high in the air.

Farmer Tucci had two kinds of goats. He had milk goats and pack goats. The pack goats were much bigger than milk goats and were kept in another pen. The other milk goats were not French milk goats, so, other than Mimi, the milk goats and the pack goats talked through the fence most everyday. But no one talked today.

The farm was silent. It was empty. Something was wrong.

Mimi paced back and forth in her pen. She watched the sun crawling over the hills and didn't think she would be able stand a whole day of this torture. Her heart was aching for some reason, and she, like everyone else, had no idea what to do.

The pigs were digging to make more mud, thinking that might be the reason. The cows were swatting more flies thinking that might be the reason. The chickens were trying to lay more eggs thinking that might be the reason. No one knew what to do.

Then, it happened. It just came out, out of nowhere, floating across the farmyard. A voice, a beautiful voice was singing an aria, a song from the Opera. It was an aria they all knew, but it didn't come from the record player in the house.

It didn't come from the record player in the barn.

It didn't come from the record player in the shed.

It didn't come from the record player in the hen house.

In fact, it wasn't a record player at all. It wasn't the radio either.

It was Mimi.

Mimi had never heard herself sing. She didn't

even know she could sing. But her voice rang out across the pens and the buildings and floated into every ear on the farm. It floated into the house where poor Farmer Tucci sat at the kitchen table with glue, hopelessly trying to glue pieces of his broken records together.

"What is that?" he whispered. "An aria?"

"Yes!" he shouted. "Someone it singing! One record must be left!" He looked up to heaven and clasped his hands saying, "Thank you God!" as he ran outside.

Farmer Tucci ran wildly in the direction of the sound, never stopping to wonder how a record could be playing all by itself. He followed the voice passed the chicken pens, passed the pigpens until he reached the barn.

As he ran into the barn, he saw that the phonograph was not spinning. No record was sitting on it. There was no one around at all. Except a goat. A white milk goat his wife called "Mimi" was standing in the middle of her pen with her tail pointing straight up to the sky singing with a voice more beautiful than he had ever heard before.

Farmer Tucci stared and stared with his mouth hanging open so low that a fly took a spin inside, buzzed around each of his teeth, then out again.

Mimi stopped singing.

She stared at Farmer Tucci and Farmer Tucci stared back at her. Farmer Tucci did nothing for so long and everything was so quiet, that Mimi began to sing once more. This time she started singing a song that needed two singers. It was a "duet", (which is a song two people sing together).

Mimi sang the girl part and when it came to the part where someone else was supposed to sing, she stopped and waited. After the other singing part was over, she sang the girl part again. This went on until she reached the end of the duet. She stopped singing and stood there, looking at Farmer Tucci.

Farmer Tucci started to shake all over, sank to his knees, turned his face to the sky, crying and praying, thanking God for sending him such a miracle.

Mimi sang the duet again, singing the girl part and waiting in silence where someone else was supposed to sing.

Suddenly ANOTHER voice came in singing the other part!

Farmer Tucci's eyes nearly popped out of his head when he saw one of the Spanish pack goats standing on it's hind legs, leaning over the fence to see Mimi! It was the black goat Farmer Tucci's wife called, "Rudolfo".

Rudolfo was singing at the top of his goat lungs, his neck stretched and his horns pointing straight up. It was a beautiful voice! A glorious voice! And Farmer Tucci prayed even louder now, thanking God for sending him TWO miracle goats!

Mimi was surprised to hear another voice, and stood up, leaning on the fence to face Rudolfo. They stood there, the fence between them, singing as if they had done it all their lives. It was the most beautiful duet Farmer Tucci had ever heard. There wasn't any music playing with them of course, but it was better than any record he had ever owned! Farmer Tucci stayed there, on his knees, swaying to their beautiful voices as Mimi and Rudolfo sang on and on.

The other animals swayed too. They were so happy to have music again! The world seemed right! The farm felt like their perfect old farm again! Even the prize- winning pigs felt relieved and happy.

All, but one.

Bernardo was a reddish brown pig that had won many prizes for Farmer Tucci. He was in the best shape of any of the pigs, which meant he was by far the fattest.

Bernardo believed that the Tucci farm was a pig farm. It was a farm for the pigs. The other animals were there just to liven up the place a bit and make the neighbors think that Farmer Tucci cared about animals other than pigs. Bernardo didn't believe that.

"How could you care about animals other than pigs?" Bernardo thought with his sing-song Italian accent. "What-uh is-uh there to care about? They aren't-uh fat. They don't-uh win prizes, at least not good-uh ones. They don't even eat-uh slushy sloppy-uh food. So, why bother to care about them? Pigs...now, pigs are the reason there is a farm at all-uh."

Something was happening in the barn Bernardo didn't like. Farmer Tucci had never gotten down on his knees and prayed in front of him, Bernardo, his most prize- winning pig. Why should he for a goat?

"What'suh the biguh deal?" he grunted. "A goat does one-uh little-uh thing. So what?" He looked again at Farmer Tucci, who was on his knees, hands clasped looking heavenward.

"This is not-uh good, I think," he grunted. "Maybe Farmer the Tucci, he is crazy in-uh the head, huh? What if..." he thought, "what if-uh these goats start winning-uh prizes? Start getting blessed in-uh the church? Start getting pictures in-uh the paper? What happens then? What happens to me, the great-uh Bernardo? Maybe Farmer the Tucci, don't like me so much then? Maybe Farmer the Tucci, he forget about-uh Bernardo and the pigs. Maybe instead of a pig-uh farm, Farmer the Tucci start a "goat-uh" farm, eh? Ugh! I don't-uh even-uh wanna think about it! That's-uh sick!"

And Bernardo glared at the other pigs in his pen. Through his piggy little yellow eyes he could see that the other pigs were perfectly happy listening to Mimi and Rudolfo sing. They weren't as smart as Bernardo. They didn't see the danger. "Stupido pigs," he grunted as he stared through the railings of his pen, "they don't-uh understand nothing! But I, Bernardo, I understand-uh and let-uh me tell you, it-uh stinks!"

CHAPTER THREE

That very day, Farmer Tucci went into town and bought more opera records. But these were different records. No one sang on these records. These records were just the music. He brought the records home, put the phonograph player next to the goat pens, and turned it on.

The music started playing just like the old days, but there were no voices with the music. Again, Mimi felt this was terribly wrong.

"There must be singing with such great and beautiful music as zees", she thought with her French accent. And so she began to sing.

The pack goat, Rudolfo feeling the same way, sang too. He didn't know why he sang. It just came out. He knew where the singing should go and when to stop, how high it went and how low, he even knew when to sing softly and when to sing louder. And he knew all this without even thinking. So he didn't think about singing. He thought about Mimi.

Rudolfo had never spoken to Mimi. Any time

he or the other goats came near her she would look away and stick her nose in the air.

"She is like a queen", he thought to himself with his Spanish accent. Every day Rudolfo would stare at her through the rails of the fence as he chewed his hay. "I am big and clumsy and not too clever for her to notice me. But I notice her…and I notice her…and I notice her." Rudolfo would just sigh, as he sighed every day while he was noticing Mimi and chewed his hay.

That week, strangers came to the Tucci Farm.

People came from the newspapers.

The Mayor of the village came to get his picture taken next to Mimi and Rudolfo.

Priests from the church came, sprinkling water on the two goats.

Lots of people came, all of them streaming by the pens where Mimi and Rudolfo sang aria after aria and sometimes duets, stopping only to chew a little hay.

No one visited Bernardo.

"They used to sprinkle me!" grunted Bernardo. "They used to take-uh pictures of me, the great-uh Bernardo! Soon maybe Farmer the Tucci, he sell-uh the pigs! Bernardo too!" Bernardo thought and thought about this problem as he slurped up slop from the pig trough and let it run slowly down his chin.

He was just as good as any goat. In fact, pigs were much better than goats. Everyone knew that. They were much better than any animal on the farm. They were the smartest barnyard animal. They were artists. What other animal could cover themselves with as much mud, or splash as much food on their faces while they ate?

"Why, if I wanted to", he thought, glaring off in the direction of the goat pens, "I could-uh sing too. I, Bernardo, could-uh sing more better than those stupido goats!" And, in a terrible mood, Bernardo shoved his snout into the trough and slurped up so much slop it made him burp.

CHAPTER FOUR

The next day people from the radio came to the farm.

Farmer Tucci put on his suit and Marta put on her best dress, (which was a hard decision because she only had two good dresses). The radio people brought a microphone and put it next to the goat pens and Farmer Tucci started the phonograph player. But before the music could even get started, another voice came booming across the yard!

Farmer Tucci picked up the needle from the record as he, Marta and the people from the radio listened. The big low voice came again and while the people from the radio stared at each other, Farmer Tucci ran toward the pigpens. When he reached the fence, Farmer Tucci saw the strangest sight he had ever seen! It was a stranger sight than anyone in the whole world had ever seen!

There in the middle of the muddy, stinky pigpen, sat his prize pig, Bernardo, singing.

Bernardo was sitting on his big fat rump, (a rump he took great pride in, by the way) and was singing at the top of his big fat lungs. It was a beautiful deep voice and he was singing an aria the animals had heard many times before, only not being sung by a pig.

Farmer Tucci couldn't believe his good fortune.

He jumped in the air and twirled around and around then dropped to his knees and started praying, thanking God for bringing him two singing goats and now a singing pig! What kind of a farmer must he be! And who needed records and phonograph players when you had singing goats and a singing pig!

The radio people raced over with their radio boxes and wires and put the microphone up to Bernardo's pen. Bernardo squished over through the mud on his pointy hooves to the microphone and sang his song as if he had done it all his life. The radio people were amazed. To tell the truth, Bernardo was a little amazed himself. He had never thought about singing before. It's not something a pig thinks about. But now, he found he rather liked the sound of his own voice. It was, after all, a 'pig' voice. It was like a grunt, only longer. And who could grunt better than a pig? Certainly not goats.

Soon Bernardo finished his song and stood, sticking his snout through the fence, grunting at the Radio People as they gazed back at him in awe.

"Let those-uh goats try to make-uh this a goat-uh farm now," Bernardo was saying in pig grunts, strutting around the pigpen and plopping down in a puddle of water. "Look at them", he thought as he glanced at the Radio People, "Right now they all wish they were pigs too. I bet they don't think about goats no more, eh?"

But the Radio People DID think about the goats. Right after Bernardo finished singing, Mimi and Rudolfo sang a duet and all the Radio People raced over to THEIR pen. Bernardo could do nothing. He merely sneered at them with his piggy eyes as smelly steam rose from his great fat body.

CHAPTER FIVE

The next day Bernardo's, Mimi's and Rudolfo's voices were on the radio.

The day after that they were on the radio all over the world.

"A singing pig!"

"Singing goats!"

"Animals singing Opera!" shouted the radios in every language.

Although this news thrilled millions of people all over the world, there was one person it did not thrill. The famous opera diva, Frita Von Frikt.

A Diva is almost like a queen. At least in her own mind. And what was in Frita Von Frikt's own mind was really all that she cared about anyway.

In her own mind, she was the queen of the opera world. After all, had she not eaten with Kings and Queens? Had she not been called the Opera World's greatest gift? Is it not true that people get trampled, limbs broken, crying, pleading just to be able to touch her gloved hand. She was, and she was sure everyone would agree, the most famous singer in the world.

And for that reason she had decided many years ago that she was not quite human.

"I'm something MORE than human", she thought. "Something much better, I think. Why else vood so many people throw flowers at my feet every night? Why else do they jump up and cheer when they see me? Why else vood I be wearing so much gold unt diamonds? I can have anysink I want. It must be..." she pondered as she stroked her chin, (a chin that was oddly similar to Bernardo's), ..."it must be because opera sing-uhs are better zan other human beings, who are smelly unt not very talented. Unt I am the best Opera singer, zo...I must be better zan everyone in zuh whole vorld, yah?"

Frita gave up thinking about this because it was tiresome. She had found that most thinking could be left to someone else less important. Even so, as she took another chocolate from one of a hundred boxes of chocolate in her dressing room, she could not help but think about something that had been bothering her. She thought once more about singing farm animals.

"Goats singing Opera!" she muttered. "How ridikoolus!

"Goats are smelly, noisy things zat people keep around zo they can make cheese or somesink." At least that's what she had heard. Frita Von Frikt had never actually seen a goat. She had never actually seen a farm. It wasn't important for her to see a farm. She knew that restaurants obviously must find chickens... somewhere, so that she could have eggs in the morning. And she knew that restaurants also seemed to find pigs...somewhere, so that she could have bacon next to her eggs in the morning. That was all she needed to know. She didn't have to actually see them. That was the job of a much less important person.

And to be honest, the singing goats didn't bother Frita that much. But a singing pig! That was different.

"Ziss is too much!" she grumbled, "Now a pig and some goats are sing-ink Opera!"

She banged her pudgy ringed hand down on the silver tray holding her tea. "How can a pig be an opera singer? How can a goat! If pigs and goats can sing opera, why, vat is to stop normal people from thinking they could sing opera too! Opera is only for zuh most gifted, zuh most talented, zuh most beautiful!" She smiled a big smile for the mirror and fluttered her eyes.

"Opera is not for smelly grubby normal people unt...pigs and goats! Why, if everyone could sing opera they...might forget how important I am. Unt then vair vood we be! This is madness, I tell you! Unt it must be stopped! But how..." She looked back at the newspaper and rubbed her chin again, smearing chocolate in long brown streaks.

There was a knock at the door. "Enter!" Frita called. A man, a very short man with a long curly moustache and lovely white suite came in the room and bowed. His moustache was so long and curly it almost hit the floor when he bowed. He had a rolled up newspaper in his hand and kept rolling it as he talked with the great Frita Von Frikt.

"Madame," said the little man twisting his curly

moustache nervously. "So gracious for you to see me."

"Yes, yes, I know. Vat do you vant!"

"Uh...as you know, I am the head of the Opera Board. And we have come up with a splendid idea to make the opera more popular than ever!"

"I am here. Vat do you need to make opera more popular zan zat?" Frita stated as she sucked chocolate off her fingernails.

"Well, we..." and he looked around just to make sure the door was still open, "we have decided to bring these famous farm animals, you know, the goats and this marvelous pig all the papers are talking about, to...to bring them to Rome and understudy the stars of our next production", he said with a big grin.

Frita looked at him, the veins in her eyes filling up so they got redder and redder.

"The great Frita Von Frikt HAS no understudy! Who can do vat I do? Nobody! Unt you vant me to be understudied by a GOAT!!"

The little man with the big moustache edged back a little toward the door. "Think of the publicity, Madame Von Frikt! Your name will be everywhere!" The man backed further away. "Either way, it is the decision of the Board, and, I'm afraid, quite final.

Frita stood.

A Jurassic shadow rose over the little man with the big moustache and he looked up at Frita with the same terror you might have if you were to wake up in the morning with a large toothy dinosaur over your bed.

"Frita Von Frikt understudied by a goat! Stepping on stage vit a pig!!" She began desperately looking for things to throw. The little man with the big moustache squealed and took off for the door.

"It is final!" he yelled.

"Never!" Frita boomed after him as a glass lamp she threw burst against the wall outside of her room. "Never! Do you hear me! I vill never if I vas to sit on hot irons..."

Her glance caught the newspaper the man had brought spread out on the floor.

The paper headline read, "Opera Goats! Opera Pig! Farm animals become the most famous singers in the world!"

Frita stared at this headline in horror.

"Vat?" she said weakly, he lips quivering, "Zee most famous singers in the vorld? Goats? A pig?"

She dropped to her chair and the wood creaked under the strain. She would have reached for another chocolate, but she was far too weak. She would probably have to be spoon-fed her favorite food later on. Her favorite food was the only thing that could save her from bad moods. But just moments after it seem her world was doomed to crumble around her feet, a strange smile began to creep up both sides of her wide face.

"Zo, these animals are to understudy the Opera stars, eh? Understudy the great Frita Von Frikt?" She snickered, then sneared at one of the maids who timidly popped in to serve her buttered toast with jam. The maid left and Frita's appetite somehow found it's way back to her like a pigeon coming home to roost.

"Hmmm...yah," Frita said to herself, licking jam off her toast as it dripped into the blubbery folds in her fat neck. "Let them come. They are nobodies. They will jump at the opportunity, although I doubt if pigs can jump too high."

"We vill go into the rehearsals and see vat happens. Rehearsals can be dangerous. Terrible things have been known to happen. People can get hurt. Animals can get hurt too, I think. Badly hurt..." and she began to chuckle and snort. "Yes, let them come unt we will end ziss farm animal nonsense vonce and forever!"

Now she laughed in earnest. Her laughter was a sound few had ever heard, but now, the echo of Frita Von Frikt's laughter, that golden voice that had made her famous the world over, bounced through the dark empty opera house where even the mice looked around for a place to hide.

CHAPTER 6

Mimi and Rudolfo were very quiet. It had been a busy month and things were never quite the same on the farm since they started singing. Strange people wandered around the farm taking pictures or sticking round metal things up to their faces as they sang.

Rudolfo had been moved into Mimi's pen, which wasn't bad for him. He could see Mimi every time he turned his head. He didn't talk much, of course, because he didn't want to show her that he was clumsy and not very clever. He was sure she knew it already, but he didn't want to make a point of it.

Goats did not have to think much. They knew what they were supposed to be like just by what breed of goat they were. Pack goats were supposed to be clumsy and not too clever. Pigmy goats were supposed to be very smart, but short. Muscle-bound mountain goats were supposed to be stubborn and rude. Milk goats were supposed to be dainty and refined and so forth. And Mimi was a French milk goat. This made her even more refined than normal.

"I feel sorry for the oaf," she sighed, "French milk goats are zuh most dainty and refined goats in the world. The smartest goats. Mustn't expect too much from this pack goat or it might make him feel badly. I'll look out for him a leetle, to make sure he doesn't embarrass 'eemself too much by not being very clever."

And so, Mimi did her best to look out for Rudolfo.

Mimi always led the way when they left the pen. She always started singing first or nodded to Rudolfo when it was his turn to sing. And Rudolfo let her because, after all, she was a French milk goat, and he was just a Spanish pack goat who was not very clever. Before long they felt comfortable with this arrangement and never spoke about.

Bernardo was NOT comfortable, although being comfortable was like a religion to him. He did not mind pictures being taken of him. He didn't mind the metal things they used to put his voice on radio. But he DID mind having to share the limelight with someone else, especially with goats.

Each time Mimi and Rudolfo would sing a new duet or aria, he tried to out do them by adding tricks to his singing. He would sing as he rolled on the ground, but that only worked until he rolled into one of the fences. He tried burying himself in mud so that just his head poked out while he sang, but the other pigs kept stepping on his head and interrupting the song. He tried to sing while he ate, but gave that up when it sprayed slop all over the people taking pictures and they went away.

The trick that finally worked was standing on his hind legs.

It was hard standing on two legs because prize-winning pigs, such as himself, did not balance well on two legs, but he practiced and got fairly good at it and it DID teach him a great lesson.

HUMANS LIKE ANIMALS BEST WHEN THEY DO THINGS THAT HUMANS DO.

It was a lesson he would have etched in stone, but unfortunately pigs do not have thumbs.

CHAPTER SEVEN

One night as the animals on the farm rested and listened to opera records, there came a "HOOP" and a "AH HA!" from the house. A minute later, Farmer Tucci came running out of the door to his house waving a paper in his hand. He ran to Mimi and Rudolfo first.

"Frita Von Frikt!" he yelled. "Frita Von Frikt!"

He ran to Bernardo's pen and again yelled, "Frita Von Frikt! Frita Von Frikt!" over and over.

Bernardo was covered with mud and didn't care to move at that moment. He supposed Frita Von Frikt was some kind of pasta. He hoped so, at any rate.

Farmer Tucci ran back to the goats and said with a big smile, "The Opera wants you to understudy the stars at-uh the opera house! My-uh little goats! My-uh prize-uh pig! Frita Von Frikt!"

By this time Marta had come from the house in her bathrobe, her arms crossed and curlers in her hair. She watched her husband run around in circles and jump in the air.

"Calm down! You're acting-uh crazy! What's-uh going on-uh?"

"The Opera wants to pay us to bring-uh our singing animals-uh to Rome! At last, I can leave this stupid farm and go to the one place in the world I've always wanted to go! The Opera House in Rome!"

Marta frowned at this. She knew the many things she did not like about living on a farm. She wanted to do important things. Like.. shopping. But what would Farmer Tucci want? Going to the Opera wasn't exciting. Not as exciting as a new dress or a new sewing machine.

"And," Farmer Tucci went on, "They gonna pay us a lot of money to go there!"

From that moment, Marta became very taken with the idea of going to the Opera in Rome.

Rudolfo and Mimi did not know what all excitement was about. Perhaps it was a new fly spray, or a type of pitchfork. They looked to Marta as if she might help them understand, but Marta was playing with the curlers in her hair and smiling to herself. Farmer Tucci kept dancing around chanting, "Frita Von Frikt! Frita Von Frikt!"

This name began to wear on Marta. She began to stare at him and narrow her eyes, as if she were trying to light his pants on fire with her gaze.

CHAPTER EIGHT

At last the day came when the three animals, along with Farmer Tucci and Marta, arrived at the Opera House in Rome to begin rehearsals for the opera. They were very tired and very nervous. A special place had been made in the basement with pens and hay for Mimi and Rudolfo, and a pen with a shallow mud swimming pool for Bernardo. Phonograph players were playing day and night with the music from the next opera so it made them feel at home.

Farmer Tucci and Marta were staying in a nearby hotel. Marta made the best of things by forcing herself to do a little shopping six or seven hours a day, while Farmer Tucci stayed at the opera house. It took very little forcing.

Each morning before the sun came up, Farmer Tucci would come to the Opera House and walk Mimi and Rudolfo around the block to give them exercise. Some of the shops would offer the famous animals rolls and pastry as they passed by. Mimi would never taste any, and whenever Rudolfo did, she would look away with her nose in the air. She thought it was not proper for goats to eat 'people food'. Rudolfo noticed her nose in the air and suspected he had once again embarrassed her by doing something not very clever.

Bernardo refused to come on the morning walks. Bernardo did not like to exercise. He was afraid it might ruin his marvelous pig figure, the award-winning figure that had taken so much food and laziness to attain. So he stayed in his mud swimming pool eating french fries and pies, ice cream with cookies, chocolate dipped pretzels and sticky buns, until rehearsal began each day.

Farmer Tucci loved the Opera House.

He liked it because got to watch his favorite Opera singers practice. It was fine listening to records, but up close, their voices were more wonderful than he could have ever imagined.

None of the singers liked Farmer Tucci. They especially didn't like the animals. They thought it was a great insult to be understudied by anything coming from a farm. But Farmer Tucci didn't care. They were the glorious opera stars he had always dreamed of meeting.

He watched Berthold Swish, the famous tenor, who's hair was so perfect it seemed like yellow whipped cream swirled on top of his head.

He watched Carmen Ingot, the famous soprano, who was very thin and wore scarfs everywhere she went. Carmen secretly believed that germs all over the world were waiting to join forces in order to give her a terrible sore throat at the first opportunity.

There was also Antonio Sporelli, the basso profundo, who sang so low he sounded like, and some say looked like, a great overgrown toad.

Finally, there was Farmer Tucci's favorite, the famous Diva, Frita Von Frikt

When Frita entered the rehearsal hall each day everyone became silent as if the whole room had been swallowed by a giant vacuum cleaner. She waddled to center stage, sang a song or two, then waddled back, careful not to give the other singers too much to envy in one day. Frita Von Frikt believed in moderation. She believed in giving to others as little as possible, and in such small doses, that people got used to not getting very much.

Selfishness was an art to Frita Von Frikt, and she believed that art was something one must practice everyday.

The Opera they were to perform was called La Boheme. It was a very famous opera about being artists, and wearing scarves, and starving to death in France. Mimi and Rudolfo were supposed to be two goats very much in love, singing arias and duets while they pretended to paint and starve.

Mimi liked rehearsals. She got to dress up in beautiful dresses and wear beautiful scarfs. She liked the way her hooves would click on the wood floor. She especially liked the paintings that had been hung on the fake walls, called sets. The sets on the stage looked like real houses, only there was nothing behind them. And there were new paintings all the time on the walls of the sets, since Rudolfo kept eating them.

Rudolfo couldn't help but eat the paintings. He was nervous, at least not about the Opera. It was about Mimi. It seemed the harder he tried to be the kind of goat she might like, the more clumsy and 'not very clever' he became.

CHAPTER NINE

A week passed.

The sky was gloomy as Farmer Tucci took Rudolfo and Mimi for their usual walk at sunrise. It would be another long day of rehearsals for both goats. Bernardo did not go on the walk, of course. He was so tired from the day before, he had fallen asleep on his back in the pool of mud, his feet sticking straight up in the air. His legs were jerking every once in a while. He was dreaming of pudding.

The chef in charge of bringing Bernardo food had done a wonderful job of making fattening things, full of butter and sugar and starch and anything else he could think of that a pig might like. The taste of pudding though, was beyond anything Bernardo had ever imagined. It was so good he would stick his whole head into the fudgy goo so he could pretend he was eating his way out of it.

Berthold Swish saw him one day, Bernardo's pig face and shoulders covered with chocolate pudding, and asked, "Are you rehearsing Othello?" and began to laugh a high tweety kind of laugh. Bernardo didn't know if "Othello" was something funny or not, but when he shook the pudding off his face, splattering it all over Berthold's new white fluffy shirt, it did make Bernardo laugh.

Rehearsals for Bernardo became the time in-between eating pudding.

He would wait at his trough each morning and each night, pacing back and forth. "Where is that stupido chef-uh with-uh my pudding", he would mumble in Oink language. He liked Oink language because no one understood it but pigs. In fact during rehearsal he had called nearly every person in the opera very rude names. They didn't know it of course, which made Bernardo even happier to say it.

"Stupido!

"Dumb Ugly Poop Face!"

"Snot Bottom!"

"Doo Doo Head!"

"Donkey Butt!" ...were but a few of the rude names he called the other singers without their knowing it.

Bernardo did not like to rehearse very much. He only did it so he would get attention and because there was always pudding waiting for him afterwards. He didn't want Mimi and Rudolfo to become more famous than he. They were only goats. Winning prizes or becoming famous would swell their heads, and they had very small heads. They couldn't handle it. A pig, on the other hand, could easily handle fame. A pig deserved to be famous and win prizes. Pigs had swelled heads already.

Not until recently had Bernardo met any other creature who thought the way he did. He thought they might be things only a prize-winning pig could think. But he was wrong. There WAS someone else who thought the way he did. It was Frita Von Frikt.

Bernardo watched Frita Von Frikt every day from under a black curtain. He would shove his nose under the curtain and wriggle until his head and beady piggy eyes could see the stage. The other singers would bow as Frita Von Frikt walked in. She would take center stage, take a deep breath and sing. It was very impressive. Her fat jaws would wobble and the lights hanging from the ceiling would shake when she hit her high notes.

She walked, Bernardo thought, "Like a fat-uh sow on-uh tip toe". In Oink language this was a great compliment. He would have been surprised how many of the other singers thought exactly the same thing...although they didn't speak Oink.

Yes, Bernardo admired this human called, Frita Von Frikt. There was something about her that reminded him of... of... well, of 'him'. One time, he even thought he saw pudding in the corners of her mouth.

CHAPTER TEN

That Tuesday was the first day rehearsals moved from the rehearsal hall to the opera stage. It was also the day of the first accident.

Mimi and Rudolfo were singing a duet about how much they loved each other, while they wore scarfs and pretended to starve and paint. This was very hard to do all at once.

The Director, a big bald man from Russia with a bushy beard, wanted Mimi and Rudolfo to wait until the last part of the song, and then stand up on their hind legs for the high notes. Rudolfo did not think this was a very clever thing to want. "I do not theen theess eess a very good idea," he said to Mimi. Mimi ignored him. After all, Rudolfo was just a clumsy pack goat and not very clever.

"The smaller the feet, the bigger the brain," is what Mimi's mother used to say. Rudolfo had large feet for a goat, but then, the man with no hair and a big moustache had huge feet.

Mimi and Rudolfo tried and tried to sing while they were standing on their hind legs, but it was hard and kept falling over.

Bernardo, laying on the wooden floor, his head pushed through the curtains, could not see what the fuss was about. Standing on his hind legs was a trick Bernardo had perfected by now.

As Mimi and Bernardo started in on the last part of the duet, they stood on their hind legs. It went very well, for a moment, then, suddenly they lost their balance and fell over on the bed just as, "WHAM!" a heavy metal light came crashing to the floor, smashing the painting right where they had been standing!

The entire cast was in an uproar!

Berthold Swish could not stop screaming, "Mine Goodness! Oh mine goodness! Der lights ist falling! Der opera ist Kapoot!" after which he fainted to the floor straight away.

Carmen Ingot was so frightened she twirled her scarf around her head, covering her face, got dizzy, tripped over Berthold Swish, and landed in a heap.

Antonio Sporelli grabbed a painting, held it over

his head to protect himself as he ran, tripped on Carmen Ingot's scarf and fell onto the big potbelly he was not supposed to have, (since he was pretending to be starving to death in France).

During all this madness, Bernardo continued to watch from the wings.

Just before the crash, Bernardo was wiping pudding off his face with the curtain. He saw a little man with red hair running along one of the catwalks. Just before the crash, the little man was standing on the catwalk above Mimi and Rudolfo. Now the little man was gone.

"Maybe pretty soon Farmer the Tucci, he don't-uh have no more-uh opera goats, eh?" Bernardo thought to himself with a porky snigger. "Maybe pretty soon Bernardo is-uh the only farm animal to sing-uh the opera,?" In his mind he a vision of himself appeared on the curtain in front of him. "Bernardo, King of the Opera" said a banner over a big picture of himself wearing a crown. The picture of Bernardo turned and gave him a wink. Shocked, he shook his fat head and the vision disappeared.

CHAPTER ELEVEN

That evening, a little man with a red nose and wild red hair knocked quietly at Frita Von Frikt's dressing room door. His name was Julian Tweedle.

Julian was a stagehand. He had a twitch that made him blink one eye a lot. Quite a few girls had slapped Julian during his life because of that twitch that looked surprisingly like a wink. He learned to duck.

Julian knocked again.

The door opened.

Frita Von Frikt stood in the opening glaring down at him. She stuck her head out further, looked in both directions and dragged the little man inside, slamming the door.

"Oh it is unforgivable, I know, Madame", stuttered the little man as his twitch made his eye wink, "but I was so nervous! I've never 'done in' a goat before! Or anything else for that matter! And... and trying to 'do in' two goats makes it even harder! I was looking down at their faces right before I dropped the light and I saw their eyes and...they have beautiful eyes, don't they? Especially the white one, kind of bluish white eyes with a little touch of brown just in the corners where you wouldn't expect brown at all and—

"SILENCE! You doomkoff!!" boomed Frita Von Frikt.

"Yes, Madame..."

She slapped him saying, "Unt don't wink at me!"

"Sorry, Madame..."

"I gave you a very simple task!"

"I know! I know--"

"Unt you buggled it!"

"I know! I know!--"

"Is this the way you prooff zat you luff me!"

"Oh I do! I do!" cried the little man, "I worship you, Madame Von Frikt!"

"Vell you have a terrible way of showing it.

What is a couple of goats venn you luff somebody, humm? I fear I must get someone else."

"NO! No, Madame! You MUST let me try again. Puleeeese! I worship you!"

"I know... but zair are many people who worship me, perhaps I should spread myself around."

"No Madame! Please!" and he fell to his knees tugging at her dress, "Another chance! I must have another chance!"

As Julius Tweedle tugged at her pearl studded silk dress, a pearl from the dress fell off and rolled across the floor. He froze.

Frita Von Frikt's eyes started boiling. "You idiot!" she growled, putting a big foot on his head and shoving the little man to the floor. "Now my dress iss missing one pearl unt I shall haff to throw it away! Frita Von Frikt wears nossing that isn't perfect, and it isn't perfect now because off you!"

She kicked him.

"Now get out! And don't let me see you again oontil zoze goats ist kappoot!" And just to make her point, she whapped him on the forehead with one of the many hand mirrors on her dressing table. The mirror broke which made her even more furious.

"Ouch!! Yes, Madame! Don't worry, Madame! Good as done, Madame!" and in a flash the little man crawled out the door and was gone.

Frita Von Frikt's great bulk settled in the chair in front of her mirror. The seams of the pearl-studded dress she was wearing were stretched to their limits, like a dam holding back a mighty river, ready to burst at any moment and spill 'opera singer' all over the room. She heard a "POP!" and looked down, beyond the many rolls of fat under her chin, to see that yet another pearl had escaped and was rolling across the floor to freedom.

"I need a strudel," she said weakly.

CHAPTER TWELVE

The next day Bernardo saw the little man with the red nose about to climb the ladder that led to the catwalk above the stage. The little man had a bandage on his forehead. He gave Bernardo a guilty glance, winked, and went up the ladder. Bernardo watched the little man for a long time, then grunted and shrugged.

"Why worry?" he thought. "It is not me, Bernardo, someone is trying to kill. It is the stupido goats." So, Bernardo forgot about the little man and concentrated on the song he had to sing with Rudolfo.

The duet told about what a joy it was to be artists wearing scarfs and starving while being artists in Paris, which Rudolfo and Bernardo sang beautifully while they both pretended to be friends. Farmer Tucci had looked forward to hearing this duet.

"You watch," he said as he led Mimi up from the basement to watch, "This is gonna be so beautiful. I think-uh I'm-uh gonna cry, so I brought my handkerchief." Farmer Tucci pulled out a long towel from his pocket. He planned to cry a lot.

The duet was as beautiful as Farmer Tucci imagined, although it had to be stopped several times because Rudolfo kept eating the canvas of the picture he was pretending to paint. He was nervous because the Director, the man with no hair and a big moustache, kept waving his arms for Bernardo and Rudolfo to move back. Over and over he motioned for them to back up. Finally, Rudolfo and Bernardo were back so far they were pushing against the backdrop of Paris.

Rudolfo did not think backing up further was a very clever thing to want. "This picture is going to tear," he said in goat language. "I do not think theess eess a verrrry good idea."

Mimi rolled her eyes and thought to herself, "Zair ee goes again. Doesn't he know he is just a pack goat and not very clever?"

Suddenly, someone yelled.

Both Bernardo and Rudolfo jumped when they heard the yell, and it's good that they did, because a moment later the heavy pipe holding the canvas backdrop came crashing down! The heavy pipe missed them by inches. They ended up being covered by the heavy canvas picture of Paris, and not a very nice part of Paris either. Rudolfo bleeted out, and was uncovered by several stagehands.

As Bernardo came wiggling out from under the Eiffel Tower, he quickly looked above the stage, searching for the little red-haired man, but no one was up there. His piggy eyes darted around suspiciously. "This is-uh no good," he grunted, staring upward. "This is-uh no good-uh for me, Bernardo. Now they try to kill-uh the pig!"

CHAPTER THIRTEEN

For the remainder of the week, the animals were nearly killed every day.

The rest of the cast wouldn't even go on stage if the animals there. Each day however, as if they were watched over by guardian angels, the animals escaped unharmed. And each new day the little red-haired man with the twitching eye would show up for work with a new bandage on his forehead.

Mimi missed her life on the farm. She liked to sing. She liked the dresses she wore. She liked the scarfs.

But things were not the way they were supposed to be. She had almost been killed by one of those things that hands above the stage and shines like the sun. And then Rudolfo and that horrible pig, Bernardo, had almost been killed by the backdrop. Mimi had almost been killed other accidents too. And worse yet, Rudolfo had been right each time!

He wasn't supposed to be right.

He was a Spanish pack goat!

Pack goats are supposed to be clumsy and not very clever.

"He isn't even a milk goat, how can he be right and everyone else be wrong?" Then she thought, "He doesn't even seem very clumsy. Perhaps it is a trick? Perhaps this is his "not very clumsy" way of making me think he is not very clumsy?"

She watched Rudolfo in the corner of the pen chewing his hay.

"He is very kind," she thought. "And, he is strong and he has a beautiful voice." For a moment Mimi imagined what it would be like to be back on the farm, Rudolfo next to her, the records playing, all the other animals happy and going on about their lives. She shook the thought out of her head.

"Mimi! It eez ridiculous!" she scolded herself, "He eez a pack goat. His kind should be in the mountains carrying heavy... I don't know... heavy 'pack' things. I am a French milk goat and French milk goats are zee best goats in the world. Everyone always said so." At least all the French milk goats she had ever known had said so.

"French milk goats are very proper and high class and belong on only proper farms," she said to herself with her nose pointing in the air. But she would never go back to the farm now, she knew. Once opening night came and she sang, they could never go back. Animals don't understand much. They don't mind not understanding. But humans can't stand not understanding, or not knowing how things work. They didn't understand how farm animals could sing. And for that reason, they would never let she and Rudolfo alone. Not after opening night. Not ever.

CHAPTER FOURTEEN

The next day Bernardo was scheduled to rehearse his duet with Frita Von Frikt. He was not eager to go. It was fine when it was only dangerous for the goats. No one would miss them. They never won any prizes or anything, but now that it was dangerous for him, a prize-winning pig, things were different. He would be missed. Farmer Tucci would miss him. And, he would most definitely miss himself.

Not only was this the day Bernardo and Frita Von Frikt were to rehearse, but it was also the day to try out make-up. The man doing his make-up made Bernardo's eyes very dark and mysterious. He made his pig eyelashes long, his pig nose pinker, wiped most of the pudding off his mouth, and added a little light red lipstick to his lips.

Farmer Tucci could not wait for this rehearsal. His Bernardo, his prize-winning pig and his favorite opera star, together, singing a duet. If it had been something he could have dreamed, it would have been a dream come true. He was so excited he brought Mimi and Rudolfo up from the basement to watch. Marta was busy putting in another hard day of shopping, so she could not able to join them.

Frita Von Frikt was late for the rehearsal, as usual. She waited until the rest of the cast was removed from the stage. That way only a few people would see her singing with a pig. She was in a foul mood.

"How can BACON be musical?" she grumbled as she walked across stage to Bernardo. "Unt how can SAUSAGE sing!" She reached center stage and stood tapping her foot, refusing to look at Bernardo. The conductor thought she was tapping the beat of the music and started.

As the duet began, Bernardo stood up on his hind legs and began to sing. He actually had a beautiful bass voice, Frita had to admit. She still didn't look at him though, that would be beneath her, but the sound of his voice was deliciously rich and vibrated through her whole body. Usually she never noticed anyone else's voice because she was too busy listening to how wonderful her own voice was. This pig also had the most pleasing smell about him. It reminded her of something, but she couldn't quite place it.

Rudolfo was frowning at something. Farmer Tucci didn't notice, but then again, he was human. Mimi could see it right away and said to Rudolfo, "What is it NOW?"

"Sometheen does not look right to me," he said in his Spanish accent. "There eez sometheen wrong weeth that wall, I theen."

"Listen to me!" Mimi said, glaring at him, "you are a pack goat. Do you hear me? You don't know anything about anything! You are clumsy and-and-and not very clever! And...and... you are making me angry wees all thees' 'I do not theen' beezness! No one cares what you think!"

Farmer Tucci leaned in to the two of them. "Shooosh!" he said, never taking his eyes off stage.

Rudolfo continued in a goat whisper.

" But there eeze sometheen wrong with the wall, I theen..."

"Ah!" Mimi cut him off with a quick turn of her head, sticking her nose in the air. Rudolfo gazed at the floor.

When Frita sang up close, Bernardo was surprised how loud she was. Humans were not as loud as animals in general, but Frita could match any animal he'd ever known. She also had very handsome pudgy cheeks and plump folds of pudgy skin under her chin. He had never met a Human who seemed so...well, (and he hated to think it), 'pig-like'. It was the nicest thing Bernardo could say about anyone.

On and on they sang, their voices blending in perhaps the greatest duet Frita Von Frikt had ever experienced, matching each other note for note, higher and higher, until finally at the very last moment, when they both thought they could not go on—

"WHOOSH! WHAM!" The set, the fake walls that were made to look like dirty apartments in Paris, came crashing to the floor!

The set would have smashed them both flat, but the window in the huge wall was open and as luck would have it, both Diva and pig fit the shape of the window perfectly. The stage of the Opera house rumbled with the sound of the falling wall and the curtains swung out from the wind it made.

The Opera house was silent.

The Director and the stagehands were standing with their mouths hanging open afraid to move. Bernardo and Frita, were the only things standing on the stage. Everything else was clumped around them in a rubble.

Bernardo, in a daze, walked all the way off stage on his hind legs until he reached the curtains and wrapped himself round and round in them.

Frita Von Frikt stood still, the window of the set surrounding her fat ankles, making strange 'clicking' noises with her tongue.

"Click, click, click, click, click..."

Her eyes were moving in slow circles and drool was beginning to dribble out one side of her mouth. The Director climbed onto the fallen set and took Frita by the hand.

"Madame Von Frikt? Madame Von Frikt?," he whispered, but Frita said nothing. She went on drooling and making clicking sounds as he led her off stage.

Mimi turned to look at Rudolfo. Once again he had cleverly noticed something no other animal or human had noticed. Once again he had been right.

Rudolfo said nothing. He did not look at her. He slowly walked back to the basement by himself.

"He is doing thees on purpose!" Mimi bleeted out in frustration. "A pack goat is not supposed to be clever! Everyone knows this! Everyone told me this when I was little, and EVERYONE can not be wrong!" But somewhere inside of Mimi she knew that everyone HAD been wrong. Rudolfo was indeed clever.

Mimi's world was built on what everyone said. She never had to use her own brain because other goats, wiser than she, had already figured everything out. At least that's what she thought. But, what if other goats were not wiser than she. What if some of the things everyone said were wrong. That would mean she would have to use her own brain and figure things out for herself. That thought made Mimi shiver.

CHAPTER FIFTEEN

It took hours for Farmer Tucci to unwind Bernardo from the curtain. When it finally happened, Bernardo remained standing on his hind legs. Farmer Tucci put an arm around the pig and led him down the stairs into the basement.

Mimi and Rudolfo watched as Bernardo came in, walking on two legs with Farmer Tucci's arm still around him. Once in his pen, the prize-winning pig leaned against the fence and stared at the pool of mud and the bucket of chocolate pudding waiting for him in the trough. He didn't move. He didn't grunt. He didn't oink. He simply stood, leaning against the fence, staring.

Farmer Tucci studied Bernardo and shook his head.

The Opera was not as fun as Farmer Tucci thought it might be. Some of the people he had longed to meet were not very nice either. Berthold Swish sniffed the air whenever Farmer Tucci passed by, as if a cloud of bad smell had entered the room with the farmer.

Carmen Ingot would always dust herself off whenever he was near and pull her scarf up around her face to keep away some germ army that might be living in Farmer Tucci's hat.

Farmer Tucci loved that his animals were famous, that they could sing opera, that so many of his favorite singers were close enough to touch, but none of that mattered if his animals got hurt. It was much safer on the farm. He hated to admit it, but he missed the farm. He missed his phonograph players. He missed his other animals. He missed Marta too.

The Opera paid Farmer Tucci a lot of money for his animals to sing. More money than Farmer Tucci or Marta had ever seen in their lives. This did not matter much to Farmer Tucci, but it did matter to Marta.

Everyday, Marta went shopping for hours and hours and when she finally returned to their room, she was exhausted. Suddenly she had money. Suddenly she could buy things. Suddenly she had to decide what things to buy. That tired Marta out more than any hard work she had ever done on the farm.

She had deep circles under her eyes. Her feet hurt. She had nightmares about buying curtains, or pots and pans, or shoes. She would toss and turn and one night even knocked Farmer Tucci out of bed during a dream about buying and electric iron that had feet. Farmer Tucci barely saw her. He had to get up early so he was asleep by the time Marta got to the room. He missed the way it used to be. He missed her telling him to trim his moustache, or to pick up his clothes from the floor, or not to scatter hay in the house. It made him think that life on the farm had not been so bad.

CHAPTER SIXTEEN

The next day rehearsal was called off. Frita Von Frikt was not ready to sing.

This was fine with Bernardo. He was still shaky. For some reason his fat pig brain would not let him stand on all four legs. Standing on two legs had saved his life. This was something his fat pig brain would not let him forget. So, instead of wallowing in his mud puddle, he merely sat in it. Chocolate pudding didn't interest him at all until morning. He leaned over his trough slurping up pudding and thinking.

Mimi was thinking too.

Her world had changed overnight. She didn't even know if she liked hay anymore. Everyone else liked hay. Everyone said she should like hay, so she ate hay. But what if she, Mimi, didn't like hay at all?

"What if I like potatoes, or beets, or kidney beans?" Then she had a very frightening thought. "What if French milk goats are not the best goats in the world?"

The little man with the red hair had a bandage around his whole head now.

Last night, Frita Von Frikt, after she stopped making clicking sounds and drooling, had become very angry with him. It was the iron teapot that hurt the most.

"You idiot!" she kept screaming, as she battered him with the teapot. "You are supposed to get rid of these filthy animals who sing opera, not get rid of ME! Vaht were you thinkink! You almost killed me zo... zo... I vood be DEAD! Zen who vood be the most famous Diva in the world! Now get out! Unt do somezing right for a change!"

"Yes, Madame! Right away, Madame!" he said as he raced out the door, the iron teapot again making a "CLUNCK" as Frita's throw landed on the back of his head.

CHAPTER SEVENTEEN

Later, Julius Tweedle was sure he would succeed as he stood in the dark furnace room. He had a good plan this time. He was proud of it.

"This will be the end of them now," the little man said to himself, rubbing his hands together. "Nothing to go wrong this time and they can't look at me with their big eyes to make me feel sorry for them. I'll put this hose down here" - which he did, shoving a hose down a red pipe that went down into the basement; "turn on the gas" - which he did with the turn of a red handle on the wall; "lock the door to the basement" - which he did with a red key, "and wait" - which he did, sitting on a red chair.

The hose was attached to a gas line in the small furnace room. The furnace kept the opera house warm during the winter. The re-haired Tweedle, his hair poking out of his bandaged head, planned to fill up the basement with gas and do away with the animals all at once. He sat, waited, hummed a bit and talked to himself.

"At last. Madame Von Frikt, will finally know that I am her most loyal fan, more than any other fan. Her SUPREME fan. Hee hee! Oh wonderful day!"

Down in the basement, Rudolfo had not said a word since Mimi scolded him the night before. He knew she was right. Everyone had always said that pack goats were not very clever and clumsy. Who was he to say that something was or wasn't right? He had been right though. But maybe that was an accident? He just had to stop being clever, even if he didn't mean to be. Then Mimi might talk to him again.

Above the basement, in the furnace room, the little red-haired man couldn't hear anything. Why didn't he hear the animals moaning or crying out for help?

"If only I could see down the pipe into the basement," he thought, "then I'd know if they were done away with properly. What good is doing away with anything if you can't tell when you've done away with them?"

The little man got up and looked down the pipe where he had stuck the hose. He could smell the gas alright. It was a very strong smell. In fact, it was a little difficult to breath.

"If only I could see down into the basement," he thought again. "I just need a little light is all."

He looked around the furnace room and there, on a shelf near the door, was a box of matches. No doubt these matches were used to light the furnace each winter.

"Perfect!" he said out loud and grabbed the box of matches. "Now...let's see what's going on down there shall we?" He lit a match.

Bernardo was pacing in his pen.

He didn't know if it was worth being more important than a couple of goats if it meant not being alive. That would sort of take the enjoyment out of it. Plus, the basement was stuffy today. Farmer Tucci had closed the pipe in the ceiling that let warm air out of the basement.

Farmer Tucci had not been in for the goat's usual walk around the city and it was starting to smell like goats. Bernardo had an excellent sense of smell but he was very picky. The only smell he liked was his own smell. That and chocolate pudding, of course.

Suddenly an EXPLOSION rocked the basement!

Mimi screamed and Rudolfo tried to come between her and the explosion. Bernardo was knocked on his back in the mud. Bits of concrete fell to the floor and smoke filled the basement. The rumble quickly faded and the animals looked at each other through the dust, then at the ceiling.

"What was that?" Mimi asked Rudolfo. Rudolfo merely shook his head, not knowing what to say.

Bernardo got up on his hind legs again staring at the pipe in the ceiling. It was twisted and blown apart, but everything else in the basement seemed to be all right.

"This Opera place, it's got-uh too many

accidents all-uh the time," he grunted across the way to the goats.

"I doonuh theen it was an accident," Rudolfo bleeted back. Bernardo nodded and grunted, agreeing with him even though he was just a goat.

CHAPTER EIGHTEEN

The next day rehearsals were called off yet again.

Farmer Tucci arrived early in the morning to take the goats for a walk around town, but this time Bernardo wanted to come too.

It was an unusual sight. Farmer Tucci, the two goats to either side of him, and Bernardo, walking upright on his hind legs. They traveled the usual route downtown to the fountain and back again. The shop owners came out, as always, to either pet the goats or wave to them. But no one paid any attention to the goats this time. They all stared at Bernardo, walking on the sidewalk, looking very human on his hind legs.

Bernardo's rule held true.

HUMANS LIKE ANIMALS BEST WHEN THEY REMIND THEM OF OTHER HUMANS.

Shop owners were running into their shops to grab pastries and rolls, tarts and cookies, pies and chocolates and running back out to offer them to Bernardo. Bernardo opened his mouth and let them drop the delicious food inside.

Bernardo was pleasantly surprised by all this. This was always how he dreamed humans should act. These humans recognized a prize-winning pig when they saw one. This was what he had always deserved! Of course Bernardo didn't realize that it was mainly because no one in the whole city had ever seen a pig walking on his hind legs before.

When they reached the fountain, Farmer Tucci took a very long time sitting and staring in the direction of the opera house.

"I miss the farm," he said to the animals. "I miss the rooster waking us up, the cows mooing at-uh the moon. It isn't what I thought it would be. This city. The Opera. I miss the farm."

Bernardo, his fat pig brain still refusing to let him stand on all four legs, sat next to Farmer Tucci at the fountain. This was the cause of a few car accidents on the street surrounding the fountain, but Farmer Tucci and the animals didn't take notice. An hour went by and Farmer Tucci was about to start the animals back when a young man, out of breath, ran up to Farmer Tucci.

"Farmer Tucci!" the young man said, "It's your wife! S he's ill! She fainted!" Without blinking an eye, Farmer Tucci ran off with the young man, leaving the animals standing on the street.

They stood for some time trying to decide what to do. For Bernardo it wasn't too hard a choice. He walked off back toward the shops that had fed him all the pastry and sweets.

Rudolfo and Mimi did not follow. It was strange being on their own after a lifetime of being inside a pen. Mimi wandered off, hoping the Rudolfo would follow her, but too proud to turn around and look. Rudolfo followed close behind Mimi never letting her out of his sight.

Mimi walked right in the middle of the street as if she owned it, as if it were a path specially made for goats. Rudolfo was afraid one of those metal monsters on wheels would run her down.

"I don't theen walking in the meeedle of the street is too good an idea."

Mimi stuck her nose in the air and walked on.

With a "Rumble" and a "Rattle" a car raced toward Mimi. She was so busy ignoring Rudolfo she was ignoring that too. Rudolfo jumped forward and shoved her out of the way just in time. The car roared passed.

Mimi was shaken. Once again, Rudolfo had been right. Again he had been more clever than she.

"I'm sorry," Rudolfo said, "I know I am just clumsy and not too clever, but taht car… I theen it was goeen to run you over and--"

"No. I am the one who is sorry" said Mimi. "I have been terrible to you all zees time. You are not clumsy and you are very VERY clever, and also very kind. I am sorry I said those horrible things. I was wrong."

Rudolfo blinked several times, not believing his ears. Was she apologizing to him? A French milk goat telling him that he was clever? WAS he clever?

The two goats started walking once more, but side by side this time. Mimi began telling him all the things she had learned by coming to the Opera house, promising him that she would start thinking for herself from now on, no matter how scary that might be.

Rudolfo began telling Mimi things too. He told her about growing up in Spain and how he had always been told that he was clumsy and not very clever. He promised Mimi that he would stop trying to not be clever, and just be himself.

On they walked, sometimes talking about the farm, sometimes talking about the Opera, sometimes silent. By mid afternoon they arrived back at the Opera house, two very different goats.

CHAPTER NINETEEN

Farmer Tucci found his wife lying on the ground outside a large store for women's underwear. The store was a dangerous place because there was a sale going on and it was hard to keep from being stepped on. He picked Marta up and carried her to a corner of the store that was more quiet.

Marta looked terrible.

She had been shopping for days and days, not even stopping to eat lunch or breakfast. She had lost weight. Her shoes were worn. For all her days of shopping since they arrived, Marta did not buy many things. That was why she was exhausted.

As any true shopper knows, the hardest part of shopping is not what to buy - shopping is really about getting the best price for what you buy. No matter what Marta wanted to buy, she always felt there must be a better price someplace else. So, she ran herself ragged searching from store to store from morning till night until finally that morning, she couldn't remember anything she wanted to buy, and collapsed on the floor. Farmer Tucci put a cup of water to her lips, and without opening her eyes, she drank.

"I miss the farm," she said softly, her eyes still closed. Farmer Tucci nodded and gave her more water.

CHAPTER TWENTY

Frita Von Frikt sat in front of the mirror in her dressing room eating chocolate pudding, (her favorite food) and feeling very low. Normally she would have someone feed it to her but she was too upset to have anyone around. There was no spoon for the pudding so she was licking it out of the bowl, smearing it all around her mouth. She was wearing a gown that had long feathers sticking straight up all over it like a peacock that had been plugged into an electrical socket. Frita Von Frikt looked perfect picture of a chocolate pudding monster, if there was such a thing.

Her plan had not worked.

Ticket sales were up. Everyone wanted to come to the Opera because barnyard animals were about to sing. What would it be next? Camels who sing? Elephants? Singing kangaroos?

"Why are they zoh hard to kill!" she said to herself. "Zay are stupid animals...well, the pig is not so stupid. And he does have a lovely voice and very deep brown eyes and— AHH! STOP IT FRITA!" she shouted at herself in the mirror. "Zeez animals must not sing, zat is all there is to it!"

There was a knock at the door.

Frita opened the door to find the figure of a little man wrapped entirely in bandages.

"Who are you? A mummy?"

"No, Madame," a muffled voice came through the bandages. "It is I, your greatest fan!" She noticed then the shocks of red hair poking out of the bandages on top of his head.

"Oh. It's you, Tweedle! You cost me my opera, you dumkopf! You failed! Failed, do you hear me! Unt why are you dressed up like a mummy? How dare you show your face here again!"

"But I'm not showing my face--"

"Zat eess not the point! It is over! Hopeless! They vant animals now! A circus! A sinking Zoo! The vorlt does not need Frita Von Frikt!"

"No, Madame!"

"I am old news!"

"Never!"

"Worn out!"

"Impossible!"

"Washed up!"

"Unthinkable!"

"Thrown out vit the garbage!"

"Don't say that!"

"The vorlt no longer needs me to sing...." and with this she fell onto her dressing table and began to cry.

It was not real crying. It was the kind of crying one does while singing an aria or a duet. She had never learned how to do the real kind of crying. Real crying was so messy and wet it never seemed quite worth the effort. The little man in bandages put a hand over his heart.

"So long as there is breath in my body, Madame, you shall ever be the supreme Diva of the world!"

"Don't tease me. It is cruel..."

"No, no, Madame! I have a plan! A final plan!" Frita stopped whatever kind of crying she was doing and turned to him.

"Final plan?" she asked. "Vat final plan?" She reached into the air as if she were blind. "Could it be possible zair is von loyal fan left?"

"The most loyal fan, Madame! At your service forever, Madame! This plan is sure to work! Then you'll see! You'll see! Then there will be no doubt that I am your one and only most devoted fan in the universe! Just wait! Just wait!" The little man turned and ran away.

This was an unfortunate thing to do because his legs were bandaged together. There was a "THUD" as he hit the floor face first. Frita Von Frikt rolled her eyes and dabbed some powder on her cheeks as he awkwardly got to his feet and hopped out the door.

"Donkey butt," she said, looking at him leave in the mirror. Then she paused, wondering where she had heard that before. Then she shrugged and went back to eating her chocolate pudding.

CHAPTER TWENTY ONE

Mimi felt as if a great weight had been taken off her back. She laughed to herself because it felt like she had been the pack goat all along, not Rudolfo. She had carried around thoughts given to her by everyone else. That's a heavy thing to carry around, much different than just carrying your own thoughts.

Rudolfo, too, was feeling lighter. He was a pack goat. Everyone said pack goats were not supposed to be clever, so he had spent his life trying not to be. It always felt like he was lying, which was a feeling he never liked. Now, since talking with Mimi, he felt like he could be as clever as he wanted, as clever as any animal in the world.

Bernardo watched the two goats as he sat in the mud. They were acting very strange. When Rudolfo crossed the pen, he brushed up against Mimi. When Mimi started chewing hay, Rudolfo would soon be along side her. Something was going on, but Bernardo couldn't quite decide what it was. He gave up and plopped down in his sloshy mud pool. His mind relaxed in mud. And in a moment of clarity he knew that was what was wrong with the world. Not enough mud.

CHAPTER TWENTY TWO

That night, late, a candle drifted down the steps to the basement. Behind the candle was a gossamer ghostly thing that the animals could not make out at first. It was not a small ghostly thing. It was large and made the candle seem tiny. The animals were ready to panic until the face came into focus behind the candle.

It was Frita Von Frikt.

Frita didn't bother with the goats. She passed them by, dressed in her lacey nightgown (which was to be complimented for doing a wonderful job of not splitting at the seams.) When Frita reached Bernardo's pen, she set the candle on the fence post and looked in at him.

Bernardo was standing before her, on two legs, chocolate pudding jaggedly framing his wide mouth. His trough was filled with pudding. Frita looked at the pudding and had to fight a strange desire to wallow in it like a mud bath.

"I shouldn't haff come. Unt yah... it is not proper for a young girl to visit a farm animal, alone... at night... vit only a candle to protect her. But, because we were almost smashed flat in a horrible agonizing death, I did not have a chance to compliment you on your wonderful voice."

Bernardo grunted once.

"It isn't often zat I am moved by another singer."

Bernardo grunted again.

"Your voice is so powerful and rich, it reminds me of someone... oh, yes, of course. It reminds me of me."

By candlelight, and with Bernardo standing on his hind legs, Frita had to blink hard to remind herself he was indeed a pig and not a human.

By the candlelight, with the rolls of fat around her neck and her wide frame, Bernardo had to remind himself she was indeed a human and not a pig. Bernardo grunted and shook his wide fat head. Frita blinked and shook her head too. They stared at each other getting within inches of each other's face. They were looking into each other's eyes when the strangest thing happened.

"I think I'm going crazy in the head," Bernardo grunted.

"Me too," Frita answered.

Then both their eyes got as wide as their piggy eyes could get and their bodies froze.

"What did you say?" squeeled Bernardo.

"Vat did you say?" squeeled Frita.

"Why can I hear you!" grunted Bernardo.

"Vhy can I hear YOU!" demanded Frita.

"You are a human! I don't speak-uh human!" grunted Bernardo

"Unt do you think I speak PIG, you doomkopf!"

"You speak-uh the pig just fine NOW!"

"How DARE you! I vood NEVER speak pig! You must be speaking HUMAN!"

"Don't be stupido! Why would I speak Human?

Pig is better than-uh human any day of the week!"

"Vell, I NEVER!" shouted Frita. "I come here to bring you a compliment, the great Frita Von Frikt, who you should be bowing to, and kissing my feet, and you start speaking human! That's just like a pig, I suppose!   Not good for anything but BREAKFAST!"

"Don't you talk-uh to me like that! I am the great Bernardo! I win prizes you could only win in your dreams! How dare you speak pig to me! Stop it this instant!"

"I'm not speaking pig, you ham! Unt stop speaking human!"

"I'm not speaking human, you doo doo head! Stop speaking the pig!"

They were both seething with anger nose to nose, when they realized that neither one of them was speaking anything other than what they had always spoken before. Frita was speaking human and Bernardo was speaking pig. The strange thing was, they could understand each other perfectly.

Their eyes widened and they both backed up, staring at each other with new and frightened expressions. Bernardo would have run away if he had not been in a pen.

Frita, grabbed her candle and waddled away as fast as she could without blowing out the flame.

"That was very strange," whispered Mimi to Rudolfo.

"I theen the strange things, they are just beginning," Rudolfo whispered back.

CHAPTER TWENTY THREE

Morning finally came.

The whole city was buzzing because today was opening night at the Opera. The famous farm animals would be singing on the legendary opera stage. The newspapers, the radio, even people on the street could talk of nothing else. Every seat of the Opera house had been sold and people were lined up at the door early that morning just in case any ticket might be left.

Farmer Tucci had taken the animals for a walk in the morning and was very nervous as he talked about opening night. Opening night meant nothing to Bernardo. Singing was singing to him. Whoever was watching didn't really matter. They were supposed to watch. He was a prize- winning pig after all. The thing that kept bothering him was Frita Von Frikt.

"Why does he, Farmer the Tucci, the shopkeepers, the radio people, or the newspaper people not understand Bernardo?" Bernardo grumbled. "Why Frita the Frikt?" Bernardo thought so much about Frita Von Frikt that he passed right by the owners of a few shops and the owners had to run after him to give him to put rolls, or pies in his mouth.

Mimi and Rudolfo didn't talk much. They weren't walking alone anymore. Side by side they went, glad to be out together.

Farmer Tucci didn't talk either.

He was thinking about Marta. They came to Rome because he was offered a lot of money to have his animals sing. Because he had always wanted to be at the opera house in Rome. But was it the best thing? Look at all the accidents. His animals had almost been killed. And what about Marta? Was it all his fault?

When they reached the fountain he sat. Bernardo sat too. They both stared at nothing and sighed as the goats stood patiently by, softly talking about the humans or the cars going by.

The newspaper people had followed them from the opera house, their flash bulbs flashing, asking questions of Farmer Tucci and writing down his answers. They were still asking him questions still, but he didn't answer. He and Bernardo looked like statues in front of the great fountain. Each off in their own world.

CHAPTER TWENTY FOUR

Evening finally came.

The sun had gone down between the buildings of Rome. The performance was to start in an hour. All the singers were in beautiful costumes. Their faces were painted in make-up so they could be seen from far away. Some were going over music. Others were pacing the halls. Still others were singing to warm up their voices.

Mimi, dressed in a fine gown made for a goat, watched Rudolfo. He was wearing a hat with a feather and a leather vest. She knew that this would be the last time they would have a normal day. Even in the basement she could hear the ocean of people outside waiting to get in to see them sing. Since she started thinking for herself, she finally knew where she wanted to be. On the farm with Rudolfo.

Rudolfo knew that singing for this many humans was the end of the life they had known. Perhaps it was the end of the life he found with Mimi. He wanted only one thing, to be back on the farm with her.

Bernardo looked magnificent in his high collar and black tailcoat. The make-up around his eyes made his piggy eyes look like black diamonds. His nose was pink and the very tips of his ears were painted black too. He didn't really want to stay in the basement with the two goats. They were in some kind of oopy goopy lovey dovey trance that spoiled his appetite. He needed some air so he went up to the stage.

The stagehands were making last minute changes to the sets and backdrops. Lights were flashing on and off just to make sure they were set right. Women were in the house, (the house is where are the seats are), brushing off the seats with little brooms. Bernardo liked the smell of the stage. It smelled like wood and paint. He was in his usual spot rolled up in the black curtain, stage left, taking big whiffs of it when he smelled something else in the air.

Pudding.

He looked around for the pudding when out of the corner of his eye, in the dark, he saw something move. He tip-toed in the direction of the movement until he could see the shape of a man. It was a man wearing a long coat. Inside the coat was a man completely covered in bandages.

A large bowl was in front of the bandaged man and he was putting t-spoons of white powder into the pudding and stirring it around. Bernardo rolled up more in the curtain to hide.

He watched as the bandaged figure scooted the bowl of pudding over next to the stage right door where Bernardo, the goats, and the rest of the cast would be walking in. Then, the figure pulled a suitcase from under his black coat.

Hay.

There was hay in the suitcase and the bandaged figure was pouring something out of a bottle onto the small pile of hay inside. He slid the suitcase with the hay near the door beside the pudding then hopped to the wall, up the ladder, and out of sight.

Bernardo walked over and smelled the pudding. There had never been pudding on stage before. It smelled wonderful, but Bernardo stopped himself from tasting it. He was a very smart pig. Eating this bowl of pudding did not seem like the smartest thing to do. In fact, right now, his suspicions were telling him it would be a very stupido thing to do.

"So..." Bernardo said to himself, "Accident-uh my--"

Just then, the doors of the house swung open and streams of people flooded into the Opera House to find seats. A horn was tooting, which meant orchestra members were starting to arrive down in the orchestra pit. They always played their instruments beforehand, as if something might have grown inside it overnight and ruined the sound it made.

Frita Von Frikt was in her dressing room, the make-up person putting last minute touches on her face to make her look beautiful. This miracle took a lot of touches. Frita should have been thinking about the accidents that she hoped were about to happen to the farm animals, but instead, she was thinking about the pig. Understanding pig language had upset her greatly. The pig understanding human language upset her even more.

"Thank goodness," she thought, "zoon it vill all be over. No more goats. No more...no more..." and somehow she couldn't bring herself to say, "No more pig."

CHAPTER TWENTY FIVE

Finally the singers were brought through the stage right door a few minutes before the curtain was to rise. The animals came last, Bernardo in the lead. As understudies, the animals were there ready to go on in case someone suddenly took sick or became injured. Most of the time, understudies do not go on. Mostly they are simply paid to wait around.

As they 'waiting around' in the wings, Mimi noticed a large wooden bowl behind the curtain leading to stage. As she got closer she could see that it was filled with Bernardo's favorite food. Chocolate pudding. But oddly, Bernardo wasn't eating it. He stood right beside it, paying no attention to it at all. A funny box of hay was a few feet away from the bowl. Rudolfo moved to eat some of the hay, but Mimi stopped him.

"What's wrong," Rudolfo whispered. Mimi motioned toward Bernardo.

Rudolfo couldn't believe he hadn't noticed. There was Bernardo, standing right in front of a whole bowl of chocolate pudding, not paying any attention to it at all. If Bernardo wasn't eating pudding there must be something very very wrong with it. And if there was something very wrong with the pudding, there could be something very wrong with the hay. Both goats backed away from the hay. Bernardo noticed this out of the corner of one piggy eye.

Berthold Swish did not like pudding.

He did, however, like chocolate very much. The smell of the chocolate was too tempting and, even though it was pudding, Berthold stuck two fingers into the bowl, scooped up some pudding and ate it.

The basso, Antonio Sporelli, could not stand to watch anyone eat unless he was eating too. So, Antonio dipped his fingers into the bowl, scooped up some goopy pudding and shoved it into his mouth. The animals each noticed all of this. So did the chorus. Seeing these famous opera stars dip into the pudding made the singers in the chorus think it must mean good luck. If Berthold Swish and Antonio Sporelli, both famous singers, if they needed good luck, surely the chorus needed it too. So, each member of the chorus dipped their fingers into the pudding until there was only a smear of pudding left in the bowl.

Carmen Ingot did not eat very much. She had always been the thinnest opera singer in the world. She had been a fashion model. Photographers loved her. In order to stay this way though, Carmen had made food her enemy many years ago. Hay, however, was not really food. How could hay make you fat? Carmen did not think hay would count as food, at least for a human. So, Carmen lifted a few straws of hay from a little box, which was not far from the bowl of pudding, moved the scarf covering her mouth and began to chew. The animals noticed this too.

Out in the house, Farmer Tucci and Marta were almost the last ones to take their seats. They were sitting in the middle of the orchestra seats, right up front. Marta looked a little better. She had a new dress and the circles under her eyes were not as dark. She was still tired but she didn't care. She was embarrassed that she hadn't helped Farmer Tucci with the animals since they had come to Rome. Tonight, she wanted to be there for him. She wanted to be there for their animals too.

The orchestra began.

Frita Von Frikt, as usual, was the last one to come through the stage right door. She immediately smelled something odd. Following her nose, she found the source of the smell, only to find the wooden bowl of pudding empty. This made her furious.

"You are all PIGS!" she whispered in a loud hiss to the clump of singers around her. Bernardo found her statement distasteful. He looked up at her and their eyes met.

"Pigs?" he grunted, sneering at her, "you don't know the meaning of-uh that word!"

Frita made a "HUMPFF" noise and turned her head away, sticking her nose in the air much like Mimi used to do.

The curtain rose and the chorus appeared already on stage to much applause. The music swelled and finally the moment came for the chorus to sing. They all took deep breaths of air and...

Nothing came out.

They tried again.

Again no sound came out of their mouths!

All the women in the chorus put their hands to their chests, as if there were some magic button there that would bring back their voices. All the men in the chorus grabbed their throats and were coughing as if there was something getting in the way of their voices. Still no one sang a note. The audience began to whisper.

"It must be the pudding," Mimi whispered to Rudolfo.

"I theen so," Rudolfo whispered back.

The conductor of the orchestra was in a panic. He motioned for another singer, any singer to come out and continue the show.

Frita Von Frikt shoved Berthold Swish on stage. Berthold looked alarmed. It wasn't his time! He didn't know what to sing! The conductor changed the chorus music the orchestra was playing to the music for Berthold Swish's song. Berthold recognized this music, took a deep breath, opened his mouth and began to sing.

The singing started out normal, then it got higher and higher, like the sound of a balloon when you stretch the opening far apart and let out the air. He kept singing as his voice got higher and higher and tinier and tinier. Finally his voice stopped altogether. Berthold put his hand to his chest but it made no difference at all.

The Conductor motioned with his baton for another singer to come out. Frita shoved Antonio Sporelli on stage.

Antonio looked at the conductor and raised his hands, his puzzled frog face empty of any kind of thought.

The Conductor, panicked, had the orchestra scramble through their music to find one of Antonio's songs. They played. Antonio recognized his music, filled up his huge chest with air and began to sing.

The singing started out normal, his deep voice filling the opera house, until his voice too began to get higher. Higher and higher it went. Antonio pushed harder with the air he had gathered in his lungs, hoping it would make his voice lower, but nothing worked. Red in the face, his eyes bugging out as if he were about to explode, his voice went higher and higher until it stopped altogether. Antonio grabbed his throat and coughed, but it made no difference at all.

Without waiting for the conductor, Frita shoved Carmen Ingot on stage.

Carmen was confused at first, but once she saw the audience, she became very calm. Being before and audience was home to her. As long as there was an audience nothing could go wrong. She threw her scarf aside, filled up her chest with air, (her chest was so thin no one could tell if it was filled up or not), and began to sing.

What came out made the orchestra stop playing.

It sounded almost like Antonio Sporelli, the basso profundo, only deeper. It sounded like a moose or a tuba. The more she sang the lower her voice got until finally the voice stopped altogether. Carmen put her hand to her chest. It suddenly came to her that the army of germs she had feared and warded off for so long with scarfs, had finally found her. The shock of this was too great, and she collapsed like fallen twigs onto the stage. The audience gasped.

"The hay," Mimi whispered. Rudolfo just nodded.

Frita was beside herself in the wings, (which, remember, are the spaces on each side of the stage). She put a hand on the behind of each goat and shoved.

As the goats skidded onto the stage, bright lights made Mimi and Rudolfo blink. The audience, hundreds and hundreds of faces, stared at the goats in confusion. The orchestra was no longer playing but Mimi and Rudolfo didn't need music. They could sing their arias and duets without it.

They walked to center stage and stood. Mimi took a deep breath, looked at Rudolfo, opened her mouth to start...then stopped. She looked at Rudolfo again. She started moving her mouth, but no sound came out.

Rudolfo couldn't understand this. Mimi hadn't

eaten the hay. She didn't have any pudding. Why couldn't she sing?

Mimi smiled at him and continued to move her mouth with no sound coming out. At last Rudolfo understood. Rudolfo too began to move his mouth, both of them singing with all their hearts without uttering a single sound.

"What's going on!" Bernardo snorted and Frita looked over at him in surprise.

"They no eat-uh the pudding! They no eat-uh the hay! Hey! They try to pull a trick on-uh Bernardo... No one plays a trick on the great Bernardo!" Bernardo marched out on stage, very sure of himself, standing up on his hind legs. He shoved the goats away from the center of the stage and started singing.

It was beautiful.

There was no music, just the sound of Bernardo's deep rich voice filling the opera house. He sang and sang as he had never sung before. He was the star. He was the prize-winning pig again. It felt like the old days, before the goats, before the opera. He belonged in the spotlight. The opera house felt like home. The sounds he was making felt glorious, and he wallowed in it.

As Bernardo finished the aria, there was dead silence throughout the opera house. An usher in the back dropped his program, his whole body frozen in shock. No one breathed.

Suddenly the entire audience jumped to their feet and screamed and clapped and cheered! Some people rushed to the stage and pounded on it making the floor of the stage rumble. People threw programs, money, room keys, even shoes and socks onto the stage, anything they had as a way to pay tribute to what they had just seen and heard.

Frita was shocked. Her worst fears had come true. A farm animal had become an opera star! What could she do now? It was over. There was nothing left for her. Opera would never be the same!

Then Frita thought, "Vait a moment...how many sinking farm animals could zair be? Maybe zeze are the only ones in the vorlt? That vood not be zo bad. Unt the goats did not sing. People will think they are a fake. There is only one... a pig. Unt he does haff a beautiful voice..."

In the middle of the applause, to the amazement of the already amazed audience, Frita strode on stage singing a high note and an even greater roar came from the audience.

The conductor, sweaty and shaky, realized that he now had two singers on stage who could actually sing. The musicians shuffled through pages of music until they found the duet music. The conductor motioned with his baton and they began to play.

Some say the duet that night between pig and diva was the most beautiful opera duet ever sung. It rang through the opera house as no duet had ever done before. On and on it went and when it ended, there was such a roar from the audience that the conductor started it all over again.

Meanwhile, high in the rafters above the stage, on the catwalk directly over center stage, little Julius

Tweedle stood holding a rope that was looped around a beam above him. At the end of the rope was hanging a huge cement block. It was very heavy and his bandaged hands were slipping trying to hold the rope steady.

He was aiming for Bernardo. As soon as he had the big chunk of cement directly over Bernardo, he would drop it. There would be squished pig all over the stage and Frita Von Frikt would know, once and for all that he was her most loyal fan.

As he scooted the cement block along, he didn't notice the long bandage from his feet coming undone. He also didn't notice the bandage getting caught in the rail of the catwalk.

He scooted the block of cement further and further until it was perfectly above Bernardo. He was ready to let it go when he finally noticed the bandage caught in the rail of the catwalk. Hopping up and down to get it free, the rope slid through his hands. He panicked, grasping for rope and just before the end of the rope passed through his hands, he took hold.

The very heavy cement block was swinging now,

looming over Bernardo, then over Frita, then over Bernardo again. It was too heavy. The rope was slipping and his sweaty bandaged hand could not hold the heavy weight any longer.

With a "ZIP!" the rope flew around the beam above, the cement block sailing to the stage below. The little man dove over the edge of the catwalk and caught the rope. His body would have followed the heavy chunk of concrete down to the stage below, but the bandages from his legs caught in the catwalk and yanked him to a halt. The block of cement stopped too, but just for an instant. Then it slipped through his bandaged fingers.

"Noooo!" the little man cried.

Bernardo looked up when he heard the scream.

A huge block of cement was heading straight for Frita Von Frikt. Without thinking, he dove for Frita, sending both of them skidding to the side of the stage just as the cement block hit the wooden stage floor.

"BOOM!" came the thunderous explosion as the cement block went straight through the floor smashing the support beams underneath the floor to splinters. "CRACK! CRACK! CRACK!" went beam after beam beneath the floor until the entire stage of the opera house moaned and shifted.

"Ahhh" came another scream, as a little red-haired man covered in unraveling bandages came spinning down from above. The bandages from his legs were still caught in the catwalk above. He was spinning so fast that when he unraveled to the end of his bandages, he spun right back up again like a human yo yo.

Screams came from everywhere now, as the audience ran for their lives. Suddenly, with a thunderous "BOOM!", the stage of the famous opera house collapsed into the basement, bringing the sets, the curtains, everything crashing down on top of it until the stage of the great and famous opera house was nothing more than dust and rubble.

CHAPTER TWENTY SIX

Months went by.

Farmer Tucci and Marta went back to the farm. Marta went shopping and bought Farmer Tucci a brand new phonograph player. Farmer Tucci bought Marta six new dresses and an electric sewing machine. Marta loved to shop, but she realized she loved Farmer Tucci much more. Farmer Tucci loved the opera, but he realized he loved Marta much more.

And speaking of love, Mimi and Rudolfo were back on the farm too. Mimi had thought for herself on opening night. She decided that she would never be able to go back to the farm, never have a happy life with Rudolfo, if she sang one note. So, she didn't. It was her smile that let Rudolfo know. He saw her smile and, being the clever goat he was, he knew she had found the perfect way for them to have the life they both wanted.

They were very happy, and they were very proud of each other. This is not to say that they never sang opera again. They sang all the time, but not when any strangers were around. Farmer Tucci and Marta would sit in two rocking chairs beside the goat pen each evening, while the breeze blew in and the crickets sang, and listen to them sing arias and duets until the moon rose bright in the sky.

Bernardo did not return to the farm.

He was an Opera star. A prize-winning opera star. Farmer Tucci had many of his records. Senor Bernardo could be seen each morning strolling down the streets of town where the shop owners would eagerly be waiting with their pastries. Bernardo would pass by, walking on his hind legs as usual, dressed in shimmering black tails, a top hat and a cane. He would open his wide pig mouth as he passed and shop owner after shop owner would drop all sorts of delicious things inside.

The shop owners had two of everything of course, because always beside Bernardo, arm in arm with the pig, waddled the famous opera Diva Frita Von Frikt. She was fatter than ever and more famous than ever because of Bernardo. They made record after record together. Wherever they sang, people would cheer and throw flowers and pound on the stage.

But, despite their fame and fortune, Bernardo and Frita kept the same routine everyday. They walked down Bakery Street, (that's what people came to call it), talking to each other in oink and human, as the shop owners and fans lined the street. They would walk with their heads held high, mouths open, so the shop owners would have no trouble popping their finest pastry into their waiting mouths. And just like everyday, a little man with red hair would be limping along behind them, keeping the back of Frita Von Frikt's dress perfectly clean and brushing away pastry crumbs. The three would always continue on, passed Bakery Street to their favorite restaurant. It was the place Bernardo and Frita lovingly referred to as "Our Place."

Outside that restaurant, fans would stand for hours hoping to catch a glimpse of the famous pair through the letters painted on the restaurant window. The letters were big and red and spelled out the name of the restaurant, a name that was well known to the people of Rome and tourists around the world. It sounded Royal in a way. A place a prize-winning pig might belong. At least Bernardo thought so.

It was called, "THE PUDDING PALACE."

ABOUT THE AUTHOR

Gordon Goodman grew up on a cattle ranch, but was composing music and singing professionally by age sixteen. Within a few years he was a baritone soloist and recording artist with symphonies all over the world. A veteran professional actor and singer, he has performed dozens of roles for the professional stage or screen, working with legendary actors and film composers. He is a professional painter, sculptor, and illustrator and creates artwork for television development projects and for institutions of higher learning. He has written many plays, musicals, and books, has two Masters degrees, a Ph.D. in psychology, has a black belt, has certifications in hypnotherapy and artificial insemination (dairy animals), and is an expert in the field of performance anxiety in humans (not in dairy animals). In addition, he teaches psychology at a performing arts college in Southern California. He has two children. His wife, formerly with the Rockettes at Radio City, is a choreographer for the Walt Disney Company. Gordon has received special commendations from both the California State Senate and the California State Assembly for his contributions to the arts.